ACKNOWLEDGMENTS

P. 1, "Muslims, what to do?", poem XXXI translated by Nicolson, R. A., *Selected Poems from the Diwan-i Shams-i Tabrizi*, Bethesda, Maryland, Ibex Publishers, 2001. P. 1, *"Love calls—everywhere and always"* from Freke, Timothy, *The Wisdom of the Sufi Sages*, Godsfield Press Ltd, UK. P. 13, "It was the time before dawn" from Lewis, Franklin D., *Rumi—Past and Present, East and West: The Life, Teachings and Poetry of Jalal al-Din Rumi*, Oxford, England, Oneworld Publications, 2000. P. 15, excerpt from "Angel" poem and p. 16, excerpt (with some changes) from "The Lament of the Reed," both translated by Nicolson, R. A., *Selected Poems from the Diwan-i Shams-i Tabrizi*. P. 16, excerpt from the "sea" poem from Arberry, A. J., translator, *The Rubaiyat of Jalal al-Din Rumi*, London, Emery Walker, Ltd., 1949. P. 21, "We came whirling," from Reinhertz, Shakina, *Women Called to the Path or Rumi: The Way of the Whirling Dervish*, Prescott, Arizona, Holm Press, 2001. P. 24, "Nobody" teaching story from Freke, Timothy, *The Wisdom of the Sufi Sages*. P. 25, "God has hidden himself in the sea" from Khemir, Nacer, *The Wisdom of Islam*, New York, Abbeville Press, 1996. P. 26, "death poem" from Lewis, Franklin D., *Rumi—Past and Present, East and West*, P.30, "God's spirit turning in us" from Moyne, John and Barks, Coleman, *Unseen Rain: Quatrains of Rumi*, Vermont, Threshold Press, 1986.

two lions

A NOTE ABOUT THE ART

Inspired by the Eastern culture of the thirteenth century, I painted the book with Turkish and Chinese inks and gold overlays. The Turkish miniatures of whirling dervishes in the Topkapi Palace Museum in Istanbul and in Konya were invaluable. I would gratefully like to thank my son, John Hitz, and his Turkish wife, Evrim Eser Hitz, for a beautiful and circular trip inside of Turkey, where we followed whirling dervishes from Istanbul to Konya and back again.   —Demi

Amazon Publishing, Attn: Amazon Children's Publishing, P.O. Box 400818, Las Vegas, NV 89140
www.amazon.com/amazonchildrenspublishing

LIBRARY OF CONGRESS CATALOGING-IN-PUBLICATION DATA: Demi. Rumi : whirling dervish / by Demi. — 1st ed. p. cm. ISBN 978-0-7614-5527-1 1. Jalal al-Din Rumi, Maulana, 1207-1273—Juvenile literature. 2. Poets, Persian—747-1500—Biography—Juvenile literature. I. Title. PK6482.D46 2009 891'.5511—dc22 2008012920

The illustrations are rendered in mixed media.   Book design by Michael Nelson   Editor: Margery Cuyler
Printed in China   First edition

Rumi
Whirling Dervish

WRITTEN AND ILLUSTRATED

BY

Demi

two lions

For children of all ages—
whirling together
in the sphere—
let's dance!
—*Demi*

Muslims, what to do? I no longer know myself! I am no longer Christian, Jew, Zoroastrian, nor even Muslim, nor of the East, nor of the West, nor of the land, nor of the sea . . . , nor Indian, Chinese, Iraqi . . . I seek the One, I know the One, I see the One, I call the One.

—Rumi, from *Diwan-i Shams-i Tabrizi*

Love calls—everywhere and always. We're sky bound. Are you coming?

—Rumi, from *The Wisdom of the Sufi Sages*

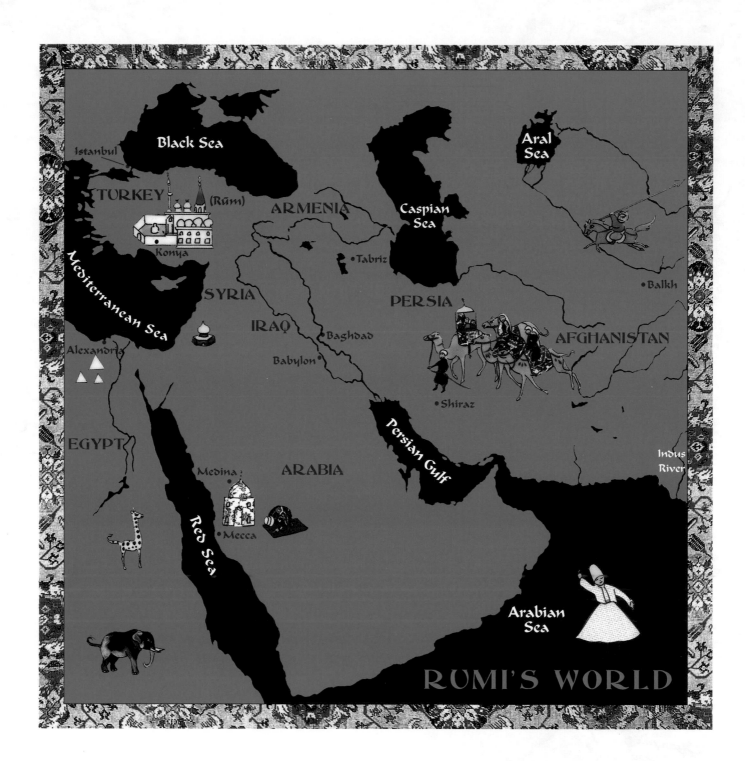

Black Sea

Istanbul

TURKEY (Rūm) ARMENIA

Konya

Caspian Sea

Aral Sea

Mediterranean Sea

SYRIA

Tabriz

PERSIA

Balkh

IRAQ

Baghdad

AFGHANISTAN

Alexandria

Babylon

EGYPT

Shiraz

Persian Gulf

Indus River

Medina

ARABIA

Red Sea

Mecca

Arabian Sea

RUMI'S WORLD

The whole world celebrated the 800th anniversary of Jalaluddin Rumi's birth in 2007, the Year of Rumi as declared by the United Nations.

Considered by many to be the greatest mystical poet who ever lived, Rumi was a simple man. He was a preacher in a small mosque in a corner of Turkey, where he once met a very special teacher. The teacher opened up Rumi's creative energies and inspired him with such a love of God and respect for Prophet Muhammad that Rumi's poetry has been unmatched for more than 800 years. The result of his life is contained in three phrases: "I was ripe, I ripened, I was consumed!"

Rumi lived in a part of the world that is now Turkey. It was called Asia Minor in English but Rūm by the Seljuk Turks. Rumi therefore became known as the man from Rūm.

Rumi's poetry speaks to the hearts of people in many lands and people of different faiths because he saw the love of God in everyone and everything. He wrote: "The practice of lovers is separate from all religions because the religion and nation of lovers is God." Rumi believed that love is the root of all religions. God is the friend and beloved of all humankind.

—Dr. Laleh Bakhtiar, PhD,
translator of *The Sublime Quran*
and author of *Sufi Expressions of the Mystic Quest*

A LONG TIME AGO,
on September 30, 1207, a boy
was born in the city of Balkh in
Afghanistan. His parents named him
Jalaluddin, "Splendor of the Faith."

His first teacher was his father. He taught Jalaluddin the Koran, the sacred book of Islam, and also the life of Prophet Muhammad, whom the Koran calls "the mercy to humanity." In addition, his father taught him Islamic law, science, and math.

Jalaluddin loved learning new things and having his father as his teacher. Then one day, when the boy was twelve, news came that a terrible warrior, Genghis Khan, and his Mongol army were conquering their homeland.

Jalaluddin's father gathered his family and friends into a huge caravan and escaped from Afghanistan. They traveled through Iran, Egypt, Syria, Arabia, and finally settled in Turkey.

Jalaluddin was now eighteen and felt it was time to marry. He met a girl from his hometown who had been traveling with his family's caravan. Their wedding was celebrated with great joy and soon two sons were born, Sultan Valad and Alaiddin. Jalaluddin and his family settled in Konya, the capital of Seljuk, Turkey.

Every day, Jalaluddin would listen
to his father's stories and hear him
read from the Koran. Jalaluddin taught
his own sons as he had been taught.
Five times a day—before sunrise, after
noon, in late afternoon, after sunset,
and at night—the family prayed. Soon
Jalaluddin was teaching many students.

9

One day a spiritual man named Seyyid Burhan came to visit Jalaluddin. He had lived as a hermit in the mountains, but when he met Jalaluddin, he was so impressed that he stayed in Konya and taught him everything he knew. Although Jalaluddin learned much about the spiritual world, he felt he had not experienced it for himself.

Jalaluddin remembered that he had spent his youth traveling and meeting great teachers in Iran and that he had made a pilgrimage with his family to Mecca. He recalled meeting a spiritual teacher who had predicted that one day Jalaluddin would come to know the spirit of God. He was now thirty-seven years old. He had become a famous religious scholar and teacher, devout and respectable, but he still had not experienced the spirit of God within himself. Jalaluddin had book knowledge but he felt empty inside. He had almost given up hope of ever meeting
a teacher who could show him the way.

Then on November 29, 1244, he met Shamsuddin, "Sun of the Faith," who was from the city of Tabriz in northwestern Iran. "Shams," a learned man with great intuition and wisdom, had traveled through many lands looking for a student who would be inspired by his teachings.

Shams taught Jalaluddin for three years. He was the best teacher anyone could ever have wished for. He said to listen for the sound of Heaven—emptying the mind of all thoughts—to hear the sacred sound of God. As Jalaluddin said later:

It was the time before dawn.
In the sky rose a shining moon.

It drew my soul from its human frame
into the sphere of spirits.

Then Shams disappeared.

During those three years, Jalaluddin was reborn as Mevlana Rumi, a spiritual teacher in his own right. Just as the spider weaves its web from within itself, Rumi began to recite poetry in Persian. Rumi had been a good preacher but his creativity was now blossoming. He had never created poetry and before meeting Shams, he had not thought much about it. But after his spirit had been awakened, he began to recite more than 50,000 rhymed couplets. He felt like he was no longer in control. Instead his creative spirit was in charge.

Rumi was able to describe angels because he said he had experienced their world.

He recited:

Whether they be like the new moon
or the moon of seven days old
or the full moon,
every angel has its rank
in terms of light and spiritual degree.
Every angel, according to its degree,
has a portion of radiance
and three or four pairs of luminous wings.

Just as the wings of our mind
amongst which there is a great difference in quality,
the friend of every human being in good and evil
is that angel whose dignity is like his or hers.
The stars shine for the sake of guidance
for the one who cannot bear the light of the moon.

One of Rumi's most famous poems, the *Mathnavi*, began with the following lines from "The Lament of the Reed."

[Listen] to this Reed forlorn
breathing [ever since it was] torn
from its rushy bed, a strain
of impassioned love and pain.
The secret of my song, though near,
none can see and none can hear.
Oh for a friend to know the sign
and mingle all [his or her] soul with mine!
[It is] the flame of love that [has] fired me.
[It is] the wine of love [that has] inspired me.
[Would you] learn how lovers bleed;
[Listen, listen] to the reed.

In another poem he recited:

Why are you envious
of this all-generous sea?
These joyous waters,
why to each would you deny?
Shall fishes treasure up
the waters in a cup?
To whom will the ocean wide
never be denied?

It was through mystical poetry that Rumi told the following story about Solomon:

When the tent pavilion was pitched, the birds came to bow down to Solomon. They found him speaking the same language of feeling in which hearts speak to hearts. To speak the same tongue is family and kinship. When we are with someone to whom we cannot confide our secrets, we are like prisoners in chains. Many an Indian and Turk speak the same tongue, and many a pair of Turks are as strangers to each other. The tongue of mutual understanding is different. To be one in heart is better than to be one in tongue.

Rumi told the story of Moses when Moses was on a journey and he lost the fish he was planning to eat for breakfast. He retraced his steps and found that the fish had jumped into a flowing stream. He confronted the fish and suddenly a spiritual teacher named Khidr appeared. Just as Shams had awakened the creative spirit in Rumi, so Khidr tried to awaken it in Moses.

Rumi spoke of Jesus as the Messiah, known by many as a great teacher who had the ability to heal the sick and revive the dead. Rumi said:

Each of us is a messiah
  in a world of people.
In our hands is a medicine
  for every pain.

Still thinking about Shams, hoping he would return, Rumi began to whirl and circle, turning 'round and 'round a pillar while his students watched. Then one day, while wandering in the marketplace, Rumi heard the sound of men beating gold.

To Rumi's ears, the sound became:

Allahu Akbar, Allahu Akbar.
(God is greater, God is greater.)

Rumi circled and circled. 'Round and 'round he went, without stopping, for thirty-six hours, until he fell to the ground. Then he began reciting his famous *Diwan-i Shams-i Tabrizi* in honor of his beloved teacher.

Rumi had felt so close to God while turning that he began teaching the circling dance to his students. They sang:

We came whirling
out of nothingness
scattering stars
like dust.
The stars made a circle
and in the middle
we dance.

Those who performed the dance became known as whirling dervishes.

Rumi's verses also turned and turned. His poems were about love and mercy as the purpose of the universe. Through his poetry, he told stories and fables and included commentary on Koranic verses. It is even said that his *Mathnavi* is the Arabic Koran in the Persian language. Whirling dervishes danced to his words, spinning out their love for God.

Rumi recited his poems only a few at a time. Students wrote down his words. In time Hussamuddin Chelebi became his favorite student and continued to write down the poems. There are 25,000 rhymed couplets in the *Mathnavi* and 40,000 poems in the *Diwan-i Shams-i Tabrizi*. Rumi also wrote a prose work called *Fihi Ma Fihi*, known in English as the *Discourses* or *Signs of the Unseen*.

Rumi became famous for his
"teaching stories" about God.
Here's one of them:

Nobody

A man knocked on the door.
"Who's there?" asked God.
"Me," replied the man.
"Go away then," said God.
The man left and wandered in the arid desert
until he realized his mistake.
Then he returned to the door
and knocked again.
"Who's there?" asked God.
"You," replied the man.
"Then come in," said God.
"There's no room for two here."

Rumi wanted children to find God everywhere in everything. He recited:

God has hidden himself in the sea
and revealed the foam.
He has hidden himself in the wind
and revealed the dust.

At the age of sixty-six, Rumi became very ill. He died on the night of December 17, 1273. As he lay dying, he told his students that this was his wedding night since he was finally going to join his beloved. Rumi passed into "union" with God. That evening, the Konya sky shone a brilliant red.

Rumi had earlier written a poem about death:

On the day I die, when I'm being
carried toward the grave, do not weep.
Do not say, "He's gone! He's gone!"
Death has nothing to do with going away.
The sun sets and the moon sets
but they are not gone.
Death is a coming together.

His tombstone says:

When we are dead, seek not our tomb in the
earth, but find us in the hearts of men.

Today Mevlana Rumi is considered one of the most revered mystical poets who ever lived. His inspired verses and his whirling dervishes show that his love of God turns forever.

After Mevlana Rumi's "union" with God, his scribe, Hussamuddin Chelebi, carried on his work. Later, Rumi's son Sultan Valad became a teacher like his father.

Sultan Valad organized the whirling dervishes and perfected the dance. He made the color of the inside robes white. He wrote down his father's teachings and created the Mevlana Mausoleum, which has a green dome, known in Turkish as *Yashil Turbe*. There, whirling dervishes continue to worship and dance to this day.

ABOUT WHIRLING DERVISHES

When whirling dervishes turn in circles, they are in a state of prayer. As their bodies spin, they believe that there is a still point in the center of their being that allows the heavens and the whole universe to join in the dance. They turn in a way that will make the Light of God descend to the earth. They believe that divine light comes through the right hand when it's turned upward. The left hand brings the light down into the world. They have faith that their turning will bring peace and love into the world.

Before the dance begins, the dervishes slowly walk around the floor three times in a circle. Each time, they kiss their teacher's hands to show love and respect for their master. Then, suddenly, they throw off their black robes as if they are releasing the things on earth that have kept them from God. Underneath their cloaks are dazzling white gowns which stand for divine light. When they spin around, it is like seeing atoms dancing around the sun. It is a heavenly dance, the dance of eternity.

God's spirit turning in us,
*   making the universe turn.*
Head unaware of feet and feet head.
*   Neither cares, they always keep turning.*